Hinting a

A collection of short fiction

Sarah Brentyn

Hinting at Shadows by Sarah Brentyn

Cover design by Rachael Ritchey

ISBN-13: 978-1539921752

ISBN-10: 1539921751

Visit the author's website at:

www.sarahbrentyn.com

To my grandmother, Grace,

who is the personification of her name.

Contents

Introduction

Playing with words sometimes feels like arranging shattered bits into a mosaic. If we look too closely, all we see are individual fragments. We need to step back to let the complete design come into focus. Writing about the fractured lives depicted in these stories gives me a sense of creating this type of art. Pieces of something that were once whole transformed into something new and beautiful.

I love the beauty of broken things. Like sea glass. Shards that have been tumbled about in the ocean. Edges are softened. Colors are muted. What was once clear is now translucent, clouded, distorting images yet still allowing light through.

This collection of flash fiction explores the human condition—perceptions, reactions, thoughts, and emotions. Hinting at Shadows illuminates some of life's darkest moments with poignant prose.

I hope you enjoy reading these stories as much as I enjoyed creating shadows with flash.

Part 1 - Mindscapes

Traveling through landscapes of the mind. Escaping into the mind. Escaping from the mind.

These stories examine the human consciousness and follow characters into a place where we can explore their inner thoughts and the worlds they've created.

Part 2 - Connections

When we talk about connections, we're often referring to travel or technology. This made me think about missed, lost, or broken connections. This works so well with the relationship stories in this section—family, friends, lovers, strangers, victims…

Part 3 - Lifelines

Sometimes we need someone to throw us a lifeline. Sometimes we just want to be heard. These are my lines about life and the voices of the characters who wanted their stories told.

Part 4 - Microbursts

Fiction under 50 words. There are some six-word stories, a few (modified) haiku, and a whole lot of micro bursting with story, all hinting at something larger and, in some cases, more sinister.

Mindscapes

Emily

Emily's hand touched sheer, silky curtains as warm breezes blew in from the forest. She giggled, running along the hallway, bare feet landing with soft thuds on the plush carpet. Her brown eyes lit up as she watched the squirrels scurry up trees.

"She's no better," Emily's mother studied her little girl. "You promised..."

"I said we would try," the doctor corrected.

"I want her back. Please. Bring her back to me."

The doctor glanced at the tiles, "I'm not sure she wants to come back."

They looked over at the girl in the hospital gown.

Emily's hand twitched. She stared with dead eyes at the playful squirrels.

Regret Has a Serrated Spoon

I just did something unforgivable.

Shakespeare says, "What's done cannot be undone."

I know the pain of this truth.

I felt the words "blind rage".

I don't remember all of what I did in my fury.

No one talks about the confusion that follows, when you're in a heap on the floor wondering what happened. Or the regret that scoops you out like a cantaloupe.

I am hollow.

How fortunate I am that regret has a serrated spoon. As an empty husk, there's a chance I can live.

With the fragmented memories of this thing that I did.

Dreams and Debris

Sitting next to the bonfire, I read the words I wrote when I still believed.

Better days were ahead. Success awaited me. Love would find me.

Flipping through pages, I watch my handwriting change. Ugly scribbles fill the diary toward the end where I wrote about the things that were lost and the things that were never found.

I want to remember, to feel something. But I can't hold on.

Bits of my life flutter in and out of my head and these memories lose their meaning. I toss the book into the flames and walk into the lake.

Go Ask Alice

When Alice was three, her teddy bear told her how to shape Play-Doh into intricate fairy houses with working windows and doors.

When Alice was seven, her Barbie doll showed her blueprints for an underwater city and she won a sand castle competition with her "Mermaid's Mansion" sculpture.

When Alice was fifteen, her parents brought her to doctors who tried to stop Alice hearing voices and hallucinating.

When Alice entered the psychiatric ward, her doctors said it would be temporary.

It was.

After Alice overdosed, they found her paintings—now in a gallery at the Metropolitan Museum of Art.

Maybe

She never had a home.

Not as an infant, left in soiled diapers. Or as a child, drawing pictures on the dusty floor of her closet.

Not even when they took her to a real house with her own bedroom, a kitchen that had food in it, and two grownups who tucked her in at night.

She was broken.

Filled with so much shame she felt stuffed. Like a guilty scarecrow with clean clothes.

Maybe they rescued the wrong girl. Maybe if they had gotten her out when she was younger. Maybe then, she'd feel at home here.

Maybe.

Crumbling

Is this sickness?

Lack of light? Solid darkness? Under canopies of lovely trees, thick with glossy emerald leaves, where sunshine cannot reach?

On the ground. Broken bits of self. Hazy eyes, unfocused from pain—grime on windows to the soul.

Shatter me.

Break apart the clumps of soil. Dig into dirt with naked hands, crumbling until fingernails become half moons of filth.

Till the earth of who I was. From this mangled mass of roots, let something whole and healthy break through. Let something beautiful grow.

This wishing. This futile hope.

Is this sickness?

The Album

She stared at the empty album, wondering again what kind of flower decorated the cover before her mind tried to find the word for the color then thought about the emptiness again.

Round and round like the seasons. In and out and back again.

Peach. It was peach, that hue. Pink. And the flower, a rose. Or carnation. Daisy. The emptiness. Pink. Flowers. Like spring. With things that are alive trying to sprout from things that look dead.

The album was closed but she knew they took the fading photos—black and white memories she was starting to lose.

Guilt

Guilt is not what I expected.

I always thought of it loud in every way. Shouting. Bright colors blinding. An abstract painting with vivid pigment and sharp edges. Unforgiving.

That's not what it's like.

It settles next to you, fully formed and alive, but smudged. Soft. Like a charcoal drawing of yourself. It whispers.

But that is all it needs do to hold your attention.

It's a powerful thing, this black and white sketch. If you listen, it will drag you into darkened corners where sunlight pools just a few feet away from the shadows. Where you have no desire to leave.

The Closet

She hadn't cried. Not when she got the phone call. Not at the funeral. But, sifting through her grandfather's belongings, she broke.

Her job was the closet—sorting clothes and shoes. It was torture.

She crawled inside and slid the door shut.

In the darkness, she hugged a plaid flannel shirt. "I couldn't find it, Poppy. I'm sorry."

Her fingers brushed the now-empty floor. The book was supposed to be here.

She smelled the familiar mix of spices and old paper.

Smiling for the first time in weeks, she opened the cover and heard her grandfather's voice.

Obsession

She squirmed in her chair at the meeting. Something about a new filing system. A co-worker glared at her. She stopped tapping her pencil, immediately beginning to bounce her leg.

Could she leave? This damn meeting had been planned for a month and her presentation was next.

Thoughts of the milk carton facing the wrong way plagued her. The front, with the cartoon cow on it, was turned toward the orange juice. She had seen it from the front door just as her son opened the fridge for breakfast.

"Excuse me," she grabbed her bag and left the office.

Bitter, Cold

I loved him with a brutal intensity.

I often wrapped my arms around my chest as one might do on a winter's morning when frost has formed where soft dew should be.

The strength of my emotions hurt and I hugged myself to add pressure, like pressing on a wound to stop the bleeding.

Without warning, that love froze. Cold seeped into my heart and, even in summer, I could never stay warm.

The shallow pond, only partly covered in ice, lets me slip into its frigid water. As I do, I wonder what will happen in spring.

Lost

She ran a brush through her daughter's hair.

"Mrs. Nevins?" the door opened a crack. "Do you need anything?"

"No, I'm…" She looked at her lap. "Silly me. I've left the…thing on the table. Could you reach it?" She pointed to a sparkly, green hair band.

"Of course." The nurse stepped in, grabbing the elastic and handing it over the bed.

"She loves this bright color. What do you call it?" She laughed. "It's kind of…ugly, don't you think?"

"I would say 'neon'. Not my favorite," the nurse agreed. "I'm calling Dr. Nate to get your meds, okay?"

"Please. Can I finish braiding her hair before the medicine makes her leave?"

The Guides

She'd always welcomed the voices.

Though Greta knew not to let on she was hearing people speak inside her head, she didn't think it was a bad thing. They were angels. Guides.

Greta wasn't a pretty girl and didn't "grow into her looks" as her mum used to say. But friends often described her as having a Mona Lisa smile.

It was the voices that formed her knowing grin. They moved with her in a steady rhythm, galloping alongside her own thoughts.

Until that one day.

The voices grew urgent, aggressive. They became a stampede, trampling her mind.

I'm Inside My Broken Self

My outer shell splits in two. It sits beside me, hollow and smiling, waiting for the next layer to be pulled apart and placed beside us.

There are six. I have six faces that are exactly and precisely me. Yet different.

Some eyes are blue, some green or brown. Some lips red, others pink or peach.

Each one me.

Each one not.

Every breath is a fissure. The thing that keeps me alive breaks me.

It cracks my next shell.

Over and over until I am small.

Human nesting doll.

Filler Flower Heart

I heard a soft voice, too quiet for real conversation, before I felt the hand on my hair. "It's time," my sister whispered.

"No," I stumbled forward and pointed. "I don't want those here. They smell bad."

"They don't smell. It's filler. Just baby's breath..." She winced.

I ran to the wreath, ripping the spray of white flowers out of their tiny, green heart and flinging the shredded pieces. My knuckles scraped the hard, floral foam.

I bled.

Someone screamed.

Arms wrapped around me.

I flailed.

Baby's breath. It's just baby's breath. No more.

Out of Oblivion

He felt the shift, if only slightly, not quite able to pinpoint when it began.

It started small, nudging him onto well-worn paths through unfamiliar woods. With growing intensity, he quickened his pace until he was running, tripping over roots and bloodying his legs.

Something was here, waiting outside this thicket of trees.

It took days of travel.

Maybe minutes.

He moved out of oblivion, traveling through landscapes in his mind until he opened his eyes and returned to the daughter he had left three months ago.

Kaleidoscope

I think I know her.

I feel calm, distant, yet my brain tells me I should be afraid. I'm sweating.

She smirks at me, her green eyes sparkling. I don't know what to think of that. I tell her so and she laughs as if this is the funniest joke I've ever told. Maybe I'm not very funny.

Then she strokes my face, long painted fingernails trailing along my cheek.

I turn away, watching my window shatter, reflecting fragmented pieces of memories—green eyes, blood. I blink. The window is whole.

When I look back, her face shifts into a Picasso painting, and I remember the kaleidoscope we played with when I was a child.

Raze the Dead

"Aren't you going to say something? Try to stop me?"

Chloe looked through the smudged window, pressing her fingers against the glass. She squinted for a moment. "No, I don't think so."

"But we're not supposed to do this," Emma slammed down the knife, her sleeve falling over raised, white scars. "I could get in trouble."

"You could get a lot worse," Chloe chuckled, "you could get dead."

"This is funny? It's your fault!"

"I know." Chloe picked up the knife, handing it back to Emma. "You know my room assignment. I'll be there if you want to talk."

The Importance of Forks

Charlie Forks liked his name. It was simple and forks were important.

Using forks kept one's hands clean during meals. This was the thought Charlie had as he unfolded his napkin, smoothed the wrinkles, and placed it gently over both legs so as not to flatten the crease in his slacks.

His cheese sandwich, trimmed of crust and cut into squares, had no mustard or mayonnaise. Charlie felt strongly that their flavor added little in comparison to their mess.

He placed a bottle of hand sanitizer on the table and his napkin fluttered to the floor.

He sighed, gathering everything, dumping it, and preparing to make his lunch again.

Need

Somewhere along the way, she lost the ability to hear her own words.

When she spoke, it sounded as if a nest of hornets had been disturbed. A hollow, distant, buzzing noise that made her head feel full of cotton.

But he heard her clearly.

He loved her and she didn't understand it. Not the love or the words.

Her thoughts were lucid, though. She watched from afar as tiny fissures formed each day—slowly shattering her mind.

She needed him to see that this life was crushing her but, though he listened with undiluted love, he was blind.

School Function

Children run. Colors blur.

Parents laugh. Voices hurt.

Teacher speaks. Words blend.

Head swells. Brain bends.

Feet stuck. Force movement. Back up. Feel wall. Touch bricks. Need grounding. Mind spinning. Not breathing. Quick gasps. Suck air.

Reach out.

His hand is there.

He grabs my sweaty palm without complaint, squeezing three times to ask if I'm okay. I shake my head.

No.

He leads me toward the soccer field. Toward quiet. He doesn't let go and so is there when I fall.

I Cannot Be

I lean, breathless, into another's arms.

I am not comforted.

Knowing I should feel loved as I'm wrapped in waiting arms carves desperation more deeply into me.

My life ebbs away, sailing from the shifting shore of my body like a piece of driftwood floating out to sea.

I'm supposed to be grateful, appreciating time, when each moment my body weakens. Each second strips me of a healthy joint, robs me of another heartbeat.

I cannot be any of the things they want me to be. I cling to self-pity when all I want to do is let go.

Fear Itself

Scott never looked in the mirror.

As he aged, grey hairs appeared among the sandy brown strands. Lines and creases formed around his eyes and mouth.

These things didn't bother Scott. He had never been afraid of growing old. The mirror showed him something else. Something he couldn't face.

It nearly killed him to see that reflection. So he didn't look.

He was terrified of many things in this world, riddled with unfounded fears. But, mostly, Scott was afraid of himself.

Years ago, Scott noticed that each day he looked a little bit more like his father.

Recess

I like going to the playground next to the school.

Especially when sand is dusted with snowflakes and swings are still.

In the dead of winter, I can be alone with her.

It's these days of quiet, bare trees standing tall, tufts of grass unmoving, that she returns to this place. She never did like groups of children running, shouting, shoving.

Drifting laughter caresses me like the light touch of a child's fingers on a mother's cheek.

In the recess of my mind, she is always alive. But, here, at the playground, she is real.

The Form

Oliver knew precisely when it started.

The nurse had asked him to fill out a form. That was eighteen days ago. Oliver had forgotten to write his street number on the address line.

Now there was a sheet with Oliver's name on it, written in blue ink, tucked in a file cabinet somewhere in that building. And on that paper was a blank spot where there should be blue numbers in Oliver's handwriting.

He had walked to the office fifty-four times with his blue pen. They wouldn't let him behind the check-in window.

He just wanted to write "1397" in the space.

Water Lily

Lily stood, looking into the lake, watching tiny fish dart back and forth in the water. It was so clear. So calm underneath.

Her reflection, distorted by ripples on the surface, comforted her.

It was nice seeing herself the way she imagined. The way a mirror could never show. An undulating form of disjointed parts continuously rearranging themselves into a girl.

Back and forth and back again.

She smiled, a genuine one that reached inside her chest somehow, unfolding pain and worry.

Tightening the rope around her ankle, Lily dropped the rock and plunged.

Connections

The Coat

He stepped through the front door, banging his sneakers to be heard above the TV.

He knew the police had phoned his dad about the mugging.

It's not like he expected special treatment, he knew better than that, but he hoped anyway.

Maybe one of those quick, awkward hugs people give like they're touching a snake. One of those would be nice.

He tensed as his father's boots sounded in the hallway.

His father stopped a few feet away, taking in the ripped clothing and black eye. His arms reached out, touching the torn, blood-stained coat. "Hope you have enough money to pay for a new jacket," he walked back to the couch.

Lady of the Lake

At the end of the dock, Phoebe dipped her toe in the lake. Her grip on the post so tight, it left indentations in her palms.

She watched the still water.

No girls floated by in bikinis, sunning themselves. No guys ran down the dock and jumped high in the air shouting "cannonball!" No children sat in the sand, slathered with sunscreen, digging with plastic shovels.

Not today.

Everyone was out walking, searching, calling. Looking for Phoebe's sister, Kaia.

They wouldn't find her. She was gone. Drowned. Of this, Phoebe was certain. She hadn't let go until Kaia sank.

Sweet Tea and Symphonies

The year before her father died, he pulled her aside, and asked her to listen to the crickets. *Summer's song*, he had called them. *Beautiful.*

They sipped sweet tea to a chorus of insects.

He asked her to close her eyes and hear with her heart.

At the time, she didn't know what he meant.

Now she sat, listening to a sound that might have been a symphony but had become the pull of a bow across the string of an old out-of-tune violin. To her, the crickets were a creaking porch swing empty of a father and daughter.

Flight or Freedom?

Kim packed her nightgown and toothbrush next to her son's tiny t-shirts and diaper cream. Everything fit in one suitcase.

She sat on the bed and looked around at what had once been her dream home.

Glancing at the ceiling, beyond which her baby slept peacefully in his crib, Kim held her husband's heart medication. She would have to wake her son from sleep. But then what?

The hotel was booked but what to leave behind—a house or a body?

She walked to the bathroom, dumped the contents of the prescription bottle in the toilet, and flushed.

Castles in the Ground

Ella fished her pink plastic shovel out of its hiding place next to the boiler.

She scraped it against concrete, pretending the floor was sand. A cardboard box full of yellowed newspapers and mouse droppings became her beach pail. She hummed and built a castle, her little hands shaping tall towers. The basement was dark and cramped but she imagined sunshine and sky.

The click of the lock startled Ella.

She froze, hand poised in mid-air, heart beating like a caged hummingbird. A creak from the first stair roused her. She scrambled to hide the shovel for next time.

Leap of Faith

She tiptoed around his moods like a drunken ballerina.

Her choreographed steps danced in and out of debris. Delicate footfalls amid the shattered remains of their relationship.

She knew when to pirouette so as not to get cut.

Practiced in the art, she executed jumps and leaps knowing exactly where her feet would land—between scattered bits of betrayal and contempt.

Home was a minefield. In those rare performances when her foot slipped, she set off explosions, creating more rubble and learning new dance moves.

Faith worked hard, living each day with the beauty of her intricate steps unnoticed.

Mirror, Mirror

She can't stand being around me. That's never been a secret in our house.

My father tells me not to take it to heart, that she's not the maternal type. It happens, he says.

I'm not exactly sure what that means but I wish it didn't happen and my heart has taken a lot.

At least I have one parent who loves me.

But I think of the way my father sighs or clenches his jaw right before he answers my questions. The way he admits my mother's lack of love for me yet doesn't try to fix it.

And then I see something in the mirror that I think might be what my parents see every day.

Splashes of Sadness

It had been three years since his sister drowned.

He sat in the gritty, damp sand, near the edge of the ocean, to prove he wasn't afraid.

No one was at the beach. Not in November. He didn't hear babies squealing or kids splashing. He didn't smell coconut-scented sunscreen or baking bodies.

But he did smell seaweed. He did hear sirens.

He remembered that day three years, five months, and seventeen days ago.

He was not alone.

Salt water splashed near him as the sirens sounded once more. Calling him like his sister. This time, he would join them.

He's Gone

"What's this?"

"That's mind your own business is what it is," my grandfather snatched the adoption papers from my hand. "Hazel!"

"Yes, dear, what is..." Her eyes widened. "Okay," she inched toward me like she was approaching a wounded dog. "It's okay."

I started crying. "Poppy?"

He held me, told me he loved me. "Those papers don't change anything."

"Gran?" I pleaded. "Daddy didn't leave me?"

She hugged us both. "He's gone."

"Where? Where is he?" I squeaked, not sure I wanted the answer.

Gran's eyes flicked to the garden. "You must understand, baby. He was not a good man."

Teetering On the Rocks

He heard the clinking.

It was a sound he knew well. His stomach tightened, heart raced. Consciously taking a deep breath, another, he walked into the kitchen where his wife was mixing a martini.

She held it out to him and winked. "It's strong."

He cringed.

"I can make a rum and coke. Or a gin and tonic," she offered.

"That's okay." Shaking, he reached for the glass.

The mouth-watering alcohol smell reached his nose. He flashed back to the bar two weeks ago. The family barbecue in June. Last night.

Turning to the sink, he dumped half the glass before his wife grabbed his wrist.

Cheerleader Spirit

Mary seemed graceful in the water—like a mermaid. The girls on the dock squinted their eyes in envy.

"Show off."

"Bitch."

"I totally hate her."

"Good thing she can't hear you. You'd be eating lunch at the loser table on Monday."

"Whatever."

Mary looked up toward her friends but found sand and seaweed. The sunlight appeared to be on every side of her. Twisting, flailing, searching for the surface, she screamed for help, taking lake water into her lungs.

"She always has to be the best at everything."

"Screw this. I'm outta here."

Without a glance back, they left.

Variations of Captivity

She stared at the dark window seeing only her reflection but knowing that, beyond the pane, he stood.

He watched.

What did he see? She wondered.

Leaving him did not give her the freedom she wanted. It was a bold move, a departure from her character, to pack up and disappear. But she hadn't disappeared. Not from his sight.

She couldn't run anymore.

The metal felt uncomfortable and cold on her leg where the gun rested.

They were facing off.

He, outside invading her privacy, taking away her sense of safety. She, inside contemplating trading one prison for another.

Closet Space

People never look up.

My parents storm in, stomp around, look left and right. Sometimes they search underneath the bed or stick their heads inside the closet.

They call my name, issue threats, curse their inability to find me. But they never look up.

That is why I hide here.

The climb is precarious but worth it. Curled up, comfortable, alone.

Relaxation washes over me on this shelf in the corner of the closet. There are always soft things here—sweaters in the summer, beach towels in winter. They won't find me.

I face them on my terms, when I am ready show myself. They are furious. But my space is worth it.

Blue Skies Won't Wait for You

"It's supposed to rain tomorrow."

He just looked at her. She tried again. "I'd really like to go outside. Get some fresh air, enjoy the sunshine."

He sighed.

"Let's go for a walk together, or a hike near that lake you love. Um, Black Creek?"

"Black Ridge Creek. Maybe tomorrow," he looked back down at his computer.

"I told you it's supposed to rain. Today there are blue skies, no clouds…" She forced a smile.

"There's only a fifty percent chance of rain," he said, not looking up. He tapped on his keyboard. "The walk can wait."

"I can't."

A Mother's Hope

"Let me help you with that," her mother smiled. She clasped the teardrop pendant around her daughter's neck. "You look...beautiful."

Hope played with the sapphire that now hung just above the neckline of her gown.

"Thank you, Momma. For this," she held up the necklace, "for so pretty dress and helping my hair get curls. I never thought me! Me! I could go to this big dance!" Hope grabbed her mother's hand and pulled her downstairs where they waited for Hope's prom date together.

He never showed. After Hope fell asleep, around midnight, her mother finally cried.

Cornered

She ran out of ink.

The damn ballpoint pen actually went dry before she could finish scratching out all the offers with her cell phone number. She hurled the Bic into the toilet and picked up her backpack.

Her breath caught as she heard the girls' room door open, laughter trickling in. It was the pack, cackling like hyenas. The same girls who wrote filth in the bathroom stalls.

"Did you see the look on her face? Priceless!"

"I know. What. A. Loser."

"Be right back—gotta go pee."

Footsteps.

The door opened.

With a Rebel Yell

He wasn't supposed to drink alcohol.

My father was a hard-working man, not afraid to get his hands dirty. Not ashamed to shovel shit for the rich folk when they wouldn't honor his degree from our country.

But he was stubborn.

I heard them argue, my parents. About his work. His genius gone to waste. His drinking.

I turned away, blasted Billy Idol from my room, tuned them out.

When my mother asked where he hid his bourbon, I walked away, picturing it next to my cigarettes in the overgrown garden.

He died young.

I smashed my stereo.

Twilight

He stands by the window, pretending to look outside, commenting on the shades of pink and orange streaking the underbellies of clouds.

But I know he is watching me.

The smell of his cologne makes me gag. Wrapped in scented memories of violence, I smile.

I am careful, casually agreeing about the beauty of the sky this time of day.

Twilight plays with light and shadow on his face.

I can see both lover and monster. This makes me wonder if the evening sunset shows him my face unmasked. The terror that hides beneath my compliance.

Stockings and Windows

My sister wakes me.

She puts a finger to her lips and we pad down the hall in our fleece footie pyjamas. It is still dark so she holds my hand on the stairs.

Our parents stand in the dining room. I feel strange—like it's snowing inside. There is quiet and cold. Our da stares at something on the floor: a Christmas stocking.

I don't understand why it's in our house. We don't have stockings. Or a tree with ornaments.

"There's a note," Da says.

My sister points to the shattered window. We are not welcome here.

Abandoned

A sudden crack of thunder sent him scurrying under the bridge. Lightning turned midnight to morning.

The boy saw outlines of abandoned cars. He tugged at his tiny boots, yanked off his sweater, squeezing rainwater from the wool. Waiting, watching, he sat in his spot.

Another crack split the air. Mama would come for him.

She promised.

One night, when the thunder was just quiet rumbling, she told him to wait for her here. Was that weeks ago? Months? He curled up, rubbing his sweater between two fingers. She would come for him. He heard soft rumbles in the distance.

Back to School

Susan sat in class as obscene rumors about her were whispered near her ear.

Nasty notes always seemed to show up on her desk. She was shoved in the hallways and tripped in gym.

School looked different to Susan than it did to other students.

Bathrooms weren't places to pee or fix makeup, they were hiding spots to catch her breath and cover up bruises. Lockers weren't spaces to keep her books, they were instruments of torture and confinement.

But Susan didn't run from misery, she gathered strength from it. And she looked forward to her high school reunion.

Setting the Bar

She was beautiful.

Stunning.

He watched the ice melt in his glass, swirling the whiskey around, just to avoid staring at her.

"Another?" The bartender held up a bottle.

He raised an eyebrow and slid his glass across the bar. "What do you think?"

"Me?" The woman walked over. "I think you drink too much."

"Yeah? What the hell do you know."

"I know you're here every day," she looked toward the dining room. "I waitress."

He wanted to tell her to get lost. Instead, he asked her to join him.

Here

When my brother died, my parents left.

They still live in the house with me but they're not here. Not really.

It's like a puppet show.

They are held up by strings, have painted expressions, and move about as if someone lifts their limbs.

If I had been the one who died that day, my parents would be here for my brother. They would take him to baseball games, buy him ice cream cones, tuck him in at night.

They would talk to him more than once a year and, when they did, they would never say, "It should have been you."

Morning Paper

She hates my youth. She hates being a mother. She hates me.

Not necessarily in that order.

She's gorgeous and not even that old. She just looks it sometimes. Resentment and jealousy have aged her far more than her drinking, which doesn't help. Her beauty shifts just under her skin so you can see it when she laughs or after a glass of wine.

When I was little, I used to think she was a vampire. I made up stories about where she went at night.

My grandpa always read the morning paper.

I'd look at the obituaries, pretending I was reading the comics, and try to figure out which one of the dead people listed she had killed. Now, in the mornings, I search for her name.

Childhood

Her treasure chest was an old shoe box, battered and torn in one corner.

It held a broken yellow crayon, a tangled necklace made from dried macaroni, two seashells, and a scribbled picture of a blue cat.

They were pieces of a happy childhood.

She forgot the name of the girl she took them from but she remembered blonde hair, always pulled into a neat ponytail, and parents who kissed the top of her head.

In the apartment she shared with her father and his gin, she rarely thought of the girl but was grateful to have the memories.

Because, now, they were hers.

The Clock

I knew I had to go home eventually.

But I was good at delaying the inevitable. Signaling the waitress for another drink, I drained my vodka tonic and glanced at the clock.

That was something I loved about this place. It had a clock. Cheap plastic, hanging on a rusted wire, and attached to a wall warped with age, it was magnificent.

I never had to take my phone out to check the time, seeing a missed call or text from her. I could say, with all the honesty of a drunken gentleman, that I didn't know she needed me.

Losing Caleb

I lost him on a Monday.

Caleb and I were digging for pretty rocks near Copper Brook. Mama packed us a thermos of sweet tea, plastic forks, and cheese sandwiches with mustard.

I don't know what the plastic forks were for but Mama always put them in our brown bag when we went out for the day.

She knew where we were. She gave us our lunch. But then she blamed me for going. For losing Caleb. Everyone blamed me. I was the older sister, supposed to be looking out for a toddler.

I didn't blame me.

But the weight of their anger crushed me.

Alone

"Will no one stand for the accused?"

Silence spread through the crowd.

Some looked out windows or at the wooden floor. Others sat up straighter, a look of superiority lighting their faces and dancing in their eyes.

All held roses. Each clutching one white and one red flower.

Petal after petal was raised in the air. Red. Red. Another red.

The large, bearded man overseeing the trial did not act surprised. "The accused will be hanged," he said blandly, "tomorrow at noon."

When the villagers arrived at the square the next morning, one white rose rested on the gallows.

Lifelines

Joint Pain

I don't have a happy place.

I saw someone talking about it in a dumb Disney movie. Can't remember which one. They're always on in the background at Sam's house.

His little sister watches those things like her life depends on it. Shit, maybe it does. What do I know? Maybe that's her happy place. Maybe that's her lifeline or something. Hell of a lot better than mine. Or Sam's.

He hands me the joint he lifted from his mum's purse. I fish matches out of my pocket and we wait for the smoke to kill the stench of neglect and the pain of our bruises to fade.

Game Shows

Mum hates TV.

When my father still lived with us, she bitched about how much he watched the stupid thing.

Now she leaves it on all day. "For company," she says.

I hear the women talk about her. How she couldn't keep a husband. I want to punch them in the face—they don't know anything.

I got my father's temper.

She's different, my mum. Fights back with her mind, not her hands.

Half the neighborhood can't pay their bills but they can see our TV glowing through the windows. They know we have power.

And can waste it.

Cocktail Party

Fruit punch splattered her dress, the shimmering silver fabric stained with neon red splotches. She looked like a walking disease. "What the hell did you do that for?"

The man smiled, wiping his large hand on a cocktail napkin. "That drink wasn't meant for you." He leaned in, tucking a stray hair behind her ear. Definitely not the woman in the photograph.

No matter. He was always prepared.

Tugging his shirt cuffs so they peeked out a quarter inch, he glanced at the puddle under her feet. "You're welcome. Now, if you'll excuse me." He patted the extra vial of poison in his pocket.

Lipstick and Radar

An hour ago, her biggest decision had been which lipstick to wear—the red or the copper. Which would look best on camera with her navy pinstriped pantsuit?

She set her face in a sympathetic yet confident mask for the broadcast.

The radar showed a Category 3 hurricane headed for Florida. Her copper-colored lips issued warnings, preparations, evacuations.

Wind intensified and changed direction, heading northwest toward Louisiana.

The storm surge would kill hundreds and there was no time to evacuate.

The school and daycare were across town from each other.

Now her decision was which child to save.

Caught Up

I watched them walk by, holding hands and gazing at each other.

"It's getting cold," the boy said, maneuvering his arms out of a jacket and offering it to the girl.

"Thanks," she wrapped it around her shoulders, "that's so sweet." She grabbed the fabric with her fingertips and tugged it around her breasts.

"Sure," he grinned and pulled her along.

I blew out a breath. They hadn't noticed me, crouched next to the fence.

I stood up and brushed off my jeans.

Fortunately for me, they were so caught up in their own world, and each other, they didn't see me behind them.

Stolen

She only stole one time in her life.

It was ten years ago but she remembered every shade of blue that decorated the box. Sapphire, midnight, and cobalt with lighter hues of azure and cornflower creating an ocean and sky.

The only other color was white, which formed a billowing sail on a miniature boat and spelled out a name.

She took what didn't belong to her. At the time, it felt right. That feeling increased as the years passed.

He blew out ten candles on his cake and smiled up at her, the only mother he had ever known.

Sickness

I remember reading about people getting sick. How, when they collapsed from fever and exhaustion, the tile was cool. Almost refreshing to put your sweaty face against.

It wasn't. It was dirty. It smelled.

The whole bathroom reeked of vomit and urine. And my head was on its floor.

There was no relief, only anger.

I didn't have the energy to stand. I was still burning hot. I had to wait for someone to find me.

And everything here reminded me of the decay inside my body.

I don't know why anyone would claim being sprawled on tile is nice.

Maybe they know that, when you're dying, your words have more power. They become important, even when they are not.

Visions

He stood breathless in his tux, staring at her figure moving toward him, her white gown almost glowing.

She was a vision.

He knew that as he scanned the slick road. Chunks of metal and shattered taillights littering the pavement.

He knew but he tried talking to her anyway, asking if she could hear him. She nodded and started crying. "I'm sorry," he choked, "I'm sorry, love. It's my fault."

She spoke but no sound reached him. She pointed to a body on the ground. It was a man in a tux.

Swayed

More died every day.

Dropping from starvation, we shuffled our feet, kicking up dust along the road. Some glanced at the tree, heavy with ripe fruit, which stood tall and untouched.

They said it was cursed.

Anyone who ate one of its peaches went mad.

I didn’t believe them.

I walked to the square, stood on my tiptoes, and grabbed a peach. I smiled, sinking my teeth into its flesh.

I don’t remember what I did but I remember the blood.

Now I watch and wait for the next hungry child to pick a peach from my branches.

The Duchess, The Daughter

I woke up at home.

My parents called lots of people. They cried and hugged me too much.

They said it had been three weeks since I disappeared.

I told them about the bears who declared war on the humans. The hedgehogs who made me laugh despite what was happening in the world. My wedding to the duke. My baby girl who I missed so much it hurt.

Now I sit in the place where Mommy and Daddy visit me. The place where people give me pills with my morning pancakes. The place where I'm six years old again.

Toddler Time

Every Saturday, Lucy walked past groups of high school kids smoking in the arched library entrance.

"Hey, Lucy! Headed in for Toddler Time?"

"Mother Goose?" they mocked.

She grinned. "Dr. Seuss today. Care to join?"

"Do we get a juice box?"

Lucy climbed the brick stairs and closed the door on their laughter.

The librarians busied themselves when they saw her. "No worries, ladies. My kind of crazy isn't contagious." Some of them had the decency to blush.

She reached the empty children's section, charred from last year's tragic fire, and smiled at the eager faces appearing around her.

Blink

We weren't fighting.

My brother and I were taking turns sledding down the small slope next to our house, being nice to each other for once. He even picked a bit of ice out of the cuff of my mitten. I couldn't grab it without taking my other mitten off and my hands were too cold.

I tucked my legs into the blue plastic saucer and went sailing down the hill. I jumped out before it stopped, stumbling in the snow, and turned to see my brother's empty red saucer glide toward me then lightly bump into my boots.

One More Night

She woke.

Noise crept into her sleep-deprived brain. The ice machine outside her room, probably. Or late check-ins dragging duffle bags. *I hate traveling.*

She reached out to the lamp beside her bed. Something moved.

She froze.

Shaking, she clicked the light on. The walls crawled. *Damn cockroaches.* Anger overtook fear as she whipped the covers back, grabbed a shoe and started swatting. *One more night. That's it.* As she dropped the shoe, she saw it was large, brown, a man's. She spun around, scanning the room.

She gasped.

A foot stuck out from under the bed.

She screamed.

I Quit

She hadn't planned to show herself.

His lungs were filling with water. She panicked, materializing and assuring him she would always protect him.

It was a mistake. He spent the next year performing stupid stunts.

~~~

"Check it out," he shouted, jumping off the bridge. "I've got a guardian angel! I can't die!"

His angel appeared, much clearer than she had the first time.

"You're looking haggard," he chuckled and rubbed the back of his head. His hand felt sticky. Glaring at her, he brought his fingers to his face. Blood. "What the hell?"

"I'm sorry," she smiled. "Good luck."
~~~

Nursery Rhymes

She crouched, hands over her ears, playground voices taunting.

"Mary, Mary, quite contrary! How does your garden grow!"

The group of giggling girls skipped away.

Mary stayed near the brick wall, shaking, imagining the torture of silver bells, the beheadings, the garden of gravestones her grandfather told her about one night when she had asked for a bedtime story.

She thought back to Kindergarten, when the teasing made her cry just because the singing of her name had sounded unkind. Now, only one year later, she cried because the images of gruesome deaths played in her mind like a slideshow.

Disintegration

The mortals' reverence faded.

They grew distracted and self-absorbed, no longer worshiping The Goddess.

Her temple fell into ruin. Crumbled bits of once-sacred stone became debris scattered among tall grass. Moss and ivy clung to marble.

She watched this disintegration as it mirrored that of civilization.

Humanity split apart like a plank of weathered wood, discarding kindness and embracing hate.

She felt no pity or sorrow but, instead, disappointment and disgust. They were a plague.

Silent many years, The Goddess waited, fury rising, until she stood and filled the heavens with her rage, unleashing a storm to end them.

Pillow Talk

She walked around the bed, her bare feet silent on the carpet. The hem of her nightgown tickled her ankles with each step. She ran her hand over the quilt, as if the patches would speak to her should she only listen hard enough.

It was the pillows. Something about the pillows. She squinted at them. What was it?

She squeezed her eyes shut, willing the thought to return. Pillows...

There were two. Propped against the headboard. Trimmed in lace.

"I can't remember!" she sobbed.

The man sat up in bed. "Did you hear that?"

"I told you when we bought this place," his wife yawned, "it's haunted. By that murdered girl. Go back to sleep."

On the Scene

"Wait!" Skinny rushed over with her can of hair spray, lifting a flyaway strand out of my face.

I sighed, "Hurry! I'm first on the scene. Don't screw this up for me."

"Okay." Skinny scurried away. "Just wanted…"

"Whatever," I snapped. "Blondie, you ready?"

Blondie shifted her camera slightly, "Go."

I drew my eyebrows together, pursed my lips, and spoke slowly. "Minutes ago," I slumped my shoulders and swung my arm to show the surrounding brown grass and trees, "our beloved park..."

"Stop. News reports coming in from everywhere. 'The dying earth' they're calling it. You're not the first…"

"Dammit!"

Dyed

Trying to get comfortable, she adjusted her head and caught sight of a single flower on the stand next to her hospital bed. Her son and his girlfriend brought it when they visited yesterday.

An unnaturally colored carnation, so obviously from the gift shop downstairs, unceremoniously plopped in a plastic cup. Hideous.

She closed her eyes on the realization that, among tubes, beeping machines, and scratchy sheets, the blue dyed flower was the only beauty in this place, despite that it, too, was dying.

Face the World

When we were young, I envied her.

She had perfect skin—like porcelain. The boys called her Snow White. The girls, jealous, nicknamed her Casper.

She was that knock-you-over kind of beautiful.

The only makeup she wore was sheer, tinted lip gloss.

After the accident, she used layers of foundation and powder she had never learned to apply. It was too thick and the wrong shade for her skin.

I've never mentioned this. Or the deep, scarlet scars showing through cracks in her makeup.

I still envy her.

From my new wheelchair, I tell her to go on without me. I'm not ready to face the world.

One of Those Days

After getting a flat tire, breaking the heel off my shoe, and cracking the screen on my phone, the heater went.

I called the repairman and made it to the post office just after they closed. That's when I noticed I lost my ATM envelope full of cash.

We spotted it at the same time, the man and I.

I, in new shoes, he, in tattered socks, dashed toward the envelope. He picked it up, looked around, and asked, "Did anyone drop their money?"

I stopped.

He stood.

I waited.

He walked.

It was the first time I'd smiled all day.

Microbursts

As I walked out of the hospital, I knew my belly might be full again someday but my heart never would.

The night moved.

Shadows formed things that crept closer toward us.

He started to run, pulling me with him. But I reached for them.

My feet brush dirt under the swing as I move back and forth.

She used to ask me to twist the chains so she could spin. Now she stares.

The prophecy was clear. The timing was vague. She wasted her life waiting, fulfilling its prediction two days before her death.

~

The world dances around my vision. I sway with its unseen music. Walk among the swirls of pigment. Live in a Van Gogh painting.

~

She blushed prettily. The sight made him weak.

He had blended so well with the humans before that.

~

"The hydrangea shrub spoke to me today."

"What did it say?!"

"Does it matter?"

"Well, no."

I heard the noise. Loud, mechanical blades that would cut my life short.

I had seen too many dandelions mowed down. Today it would be me.

~

"I love going to bars in the summer," the dragon belched. "With all those Piña coladas and sunscreen, the humans taste like little coconut cakes."

~

The waiting room, filled with angry conversations and accusations, was unbearable. She left.

Her obsession with paper clips could wait.

~

~

From the rooftop, I watched the city lights wink. They held a secret I would never know. I wasn't sure I wanted to.

~

Walking the familiar path, she stirred up a nest of wasps and a dust cloud of memories.

~

~

"Your watch is fast," she glared, limping over to the bar.

"So?"

"So?! I lost my damn shoe fleeing the ball and my carriage is NOT a pumpkin," she tucked her hair back into its ribbon. "You owe me a beer."

~

The doctors say "insomnia" and prescribe pills.

I say "writer" and pick up a pen.

~

Her voice was music and madness.

It weaved hysteric softness into a net that pulled him into her world. Into a whirlpool of tragic beauty.

He was drowning before they finished their first drink.

His silky newborn hair, scented with buttermilk, pulled me back to a brief moment of motherhood I no longer had.

~

You tell stories in the dark, smiling as your lies slither among guests. Someone flips the light, and you play victim in your own game.

~

Bringing her to the country with us was a bad idea. Her dementia worsened. We watched her eyes light up as we drove back to the city.

~

~

Multi-colored tendrils fluttered in the breeze as the dream-thief flew, stealing life-long passions, leaving humans empty and desperate.

~

Red skipped through the woods, basket swinging.

The wolf grinned. "What's in..."

She showed him the hatching eggs. He whimpered and ran.

~

~

Living shadows swirled around my body, leaving smudges of cruelty where they brushed flesh.

The sun rose, tainting my world with light.

~

He planned his apology for Saturday night. Flowers, dinner, chocolates.

The call came in Friday afternoon. Could he please identify the body.

~

"We'll take care of you now. You're safe."

The little girl looked back at her house then took the offered hand and walked away.

Watching the other kids play, he memorized their movements so he wouldn't have to tell his mom he sat on the swings at recess alone again.

⁂

The drops of blood were so round and so red. She stared at them, thinking they were too perfect to belong on a thing that was broken.

⁂

He stood by the window, lit a cigarette, and watched the newlyweds dance in their kitchen. He'd give them nine months then he'd be back.

⁂

"What's going on down there!" Zeus roared. "Mortals running amok! Overpopulation..."

Clotho glared. "Atropos lost her scissors again."

I never fit in anywhere. With anyone. Then the stars called to me. Now night lights up the darkness as I dance with my Sisters.

Deep down, she had always known this relationship wouldn't work but, when he replaced all her chocolate with carob, she finally left.

"Romeo! Wait! She's not..."

He drained the vial. "What?"

~

She slipped into her dress, lifting straps over her shoulders, kicking emptiness into the corner where it lay like a shed snake skin.

~

Eventually we learned that his rage was preferable when he lashed out. His silence meant a storm grew within him. And we would pay.

~

Tangled branches and roots reached for her.

She ran, swiping at them, knowing she could never escape the wilderness of her mind.

The quilt, faded mulberry and rose, whispered to her.

Her beauty catches me, spins me 'round, lands me in a place of madness.

I ask where I am.

She laughs. "Most ask what they are."

"Stop playing with fire!"

"But…the mortals love it. Their trees turn red, yellow, orange. The leaves glow." She pouted. "They take photos."

"You took the job?!"

"Yeah, so?"

"As the drummer of Spinal Tap?"

"Jealous?"

"I only wish I could say you're gonna live to regret this."

"Ready?"

She blew out a breath and nodded.

"You'll live forever."

They sealed her in. Icy blasts filled the tiny space, her scream lost in thin air.

I found her in fresh snow, fingers tracing circles in powder sprinkled by the gods, spirals adorning our sugared world.

Months of pretending and manipulating him. Over.

She buzzed with excitement as she finally cracked the safe.

A troll doll smiled at her.

~

They said, "If you talk about it, it will set you free."

She told them.

They locked her up.

~

"Here are your spelling tests," the teacher announced.

She walked around the room, smiling and pursing her lips, alternately.

He lowered his head, trying not to cry, knowing he'd be seeing lots of red marks. On his paper and, again, at home.

~

⁂

The end does not come in the form of bombs and flaming skies but beeps and fluorescent lights.

⁂

She heard the unsteady beat of drunken footsteps.

Grabbing her teddy bear, pen, and notebook, she hid and started on her life's path.

⁂

~

She squirmed in her chair. Something about a new filing system. Thoughts of the milk carton facing sideways in the fridge plagued her.

~

"Papa? Don't lock my door."

"Sweetie..."

"Please?"

"Ok. Just tonight."

His footsteps faded.

She smiled. "That's all I need."

~

Being able to communicate with the dead came with the unfortunate side effect of not being particularly adept at talking to the living.

It wasn't the certain death. It was the fissures of tiny tears that fractured her.

⁂

There's a monster behind her smile. A parasite, feeding off her fear and growing. She will lose. This thing cannot be slain.

⁂

I'll know, won't I?

When it's time to let go?

I watch the autumn leaves drift down from their branches. They know. Will it be that easy?

⁂

I visited his grave and, after, thought I should have brought flowers. Better still, a bottle of Scotch. I went back and we drank.

"Last call!" Noah shouted.

"Crap," the hawk sighed. "Those damn dodo birds won't make it."

"You gonna fly out?"

"I'll think about it."

~

She stepped over the dark liquid pooled on the floor, snaking through shattered glass.

This would be his last time brewing decaf in the morning.

~

She ran, barefoot in the grass, hair streaming behind her in strands of moonlit lace, searching for fireflies—nature's night lights.

~

~

The sunset was an impossible pink. Like a child had scribbled with the wrong color crayon. Surreal and slightly unpleasant.

~

As I sit, broken, birds gather food and fly to the safety of pine trees.

How natural it is that life continues. How painful.

~

~

That's when they show themselves.

At midnight.

Characters creep from shadows into my mind begging for their stories to be written.

~

Sugar and sunshine

dance in autumn. Bringing red

death to maple leaves.

She paused to assess

They mistook it for panic

Her blade flashed through them

A life lived too fast

Regrets accumulated

In hidden corners

Press "play", never "stop"

The "pause" button's for gazing

Finding shapes in clouds

She finally left

"Once and for all" she told him

He said "It's too late"

Her "Once and for all"

Was his beginning

It was the start of the hunt

A smile on his lips

And a warning in his eyes

I tiptoe through life

If I run, how far

will I get before my life

catches up with me?

Domestic goddess

Comes undone, statue crumbling

Fading into myth

If I run, will I follow?

∾

Your words fall, violent and unforgiving.

∾

She was nothing but an afterthought.

∾

That drink wasn't meant for you.

∾

Her reflection screamed, smashing the mirror.

∾

Aliens dissect humans. Discover no heart.

I learned the truth at fourteen.

No, wait! I've changed my mind.

Every first snow, I remember him.

Sometimes you just can't go back.

Acknowledgments

To my parents who have encouraged my writing since my first horror story, The Doll, when I was nine years old.

My beautiful kids (my biggest fans) who have cheered me on from the start. My amazing husband who gave me time to write, made sure I ate, brought me coffee and wine, and read, without complaint, all the drafts I shoved at him.

My college roommate and partner-in-crime, Michelle, and my psychically-linked cousin, Stacey, for their unwavering belief that I was born to be a writer.

My tweeps and blogger friends for their kindness and support.

Charli Mills who created an amazing online community, Carrot Ranch, and whose weekly prompts helped shape this book.

My writer buddies, Georgia Bell, Sacha Black, and Amber Prince, for their encouragement, honesty, and occasional kick in the arse.

Rachael Ritchey for her help and enthusiasm in addition to her vision in bringing this cover to life.

Couldn't have figured this design/techie stuff out without the ever-awesome Loni Townsend.

About the Author

Sarah Brentyn is an introvert who believes anything can be made better with soy sauce and wasabi.

She loves words and has been writing stories since she was nine years old. She talks to trees and apologizes to inanimate objects when she bumps into them.

When she's not writing, you can find her strolling through cemeteries or searching for fairies.

She hopes to build a vacation home in Narnia someday. In the meantime, she lives in New England with her family and a rainbow-colored, wooden cat who is secretly a Guardian.

You can find her online at www.sarahbrentyn.com

Printed in Great Britain
by Amazon